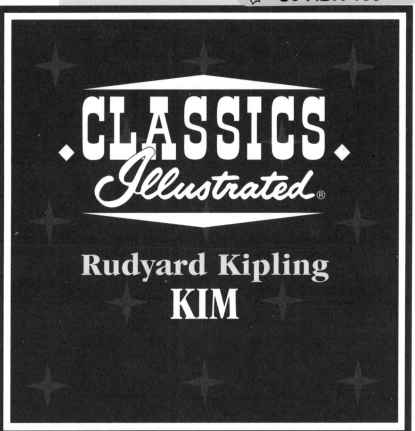

.CLASSICS.
Illustrated®

Rudyard Kipling
KIM

essay by
Debra Doyle, Ph.D.

ACCLAIM BOOKS

STUDY GUIDE

CLASSICS Illustrated®

Kim
Originally published as Classics Illustrated no. 143

Art by Joe Orlando
Cover by Vince Evans

For Classics Illustrated Study Guides
computer recoloring by Twilight Graphics
editor: Madeleine Robins
assistant editor: Valerie D'Orazio
design: Joseph Caponsacco

Classics Illustrated: Kim© Twin Circle Publishing Co.,a division of Frawley Enterprises; licensed to First Classics, Inc.All new material and compilation © 1997 by Acclaim Books, Inc.

Dale-Chall R.L.: 8.45
ISBN 1-57840-185-2

Classics Illustrated® is a registered trademark of the Frawley Corporation.

Acclaim Books, New York, NY
Printed in the United States

KIM

RUDYARD KIPLING

KIM WAS ENGLISH. HE WAS THE SON OF KIMBALL O'HARA, A COLOUR-SERGEANT WITH AN IRISH REGIMENT STATIONED IN INDIA. BUT BOTH OF KIM'S PARENTS DIED, LEAVING HIM TO GROW UP HIMSELF IN THE WONDERFUL WALLED CITY OF LAHORE.

BURNED DARK BY THE SUN, SPEAKING THE NATIVE LANGUAGE, HE LIVED ON TERMS OF PERFECT EQUALITY WITH BEGGARS AND HOLY MEN, POLICEMEN AND WATER CARRIERS. HIS NICKNAME WAS "LITTLE FRIEND OF ALL THE WORLD." AT THIRTEEN, HE LED A LIFE OF PERFECT FREEDOM AND DID NOTHING WITH IMMENSE SUCCESS.

ONE DAY HE SAT, IN DEFIANCE OF MUNICIPAL ORDERS, ASTRIDE A BIG GUN JUST OPPOSITE THE LAHORE MUSEUM.

LET ME UP!

BEGONE! RUN TO THY MOTHER'S LAP AND BE SAFE.

JUST THEN A TALL OLD MAN WITH A WRINKLED, YELLOW FACE SHUFFLED AROUND THE CORNER.

WHO IS THIS? HE IS NO MAN OF INDIA THAT I HAVE EVER SEEN.

O CHILDREN, WHAT IS THAT BIG HOUSE?

THE WONDER HOUSE. SOME CALL IT THE MUSEUM.

CAN ANY GO IN WITHOUT PAYMENT?

I GO IN AND OUT. I AM NO BANKER.

WHO ARE YOU? HAVE YOU COME FAR?

FROM THE HILLS-- FROM TIBET. I AM A LAMA AND I GO TO SEE THE HOLY PLACES OF BUDDHA BEFORE I DIE.

I AM KIM. I AM CALLED "LITTLE FRIEND OF ALL THE WORLD."

IS IT TRUE THAT THERE ARE MANY HOLY THINGS IN THE WONDER HOUSE?

YES. COME WITH ME. I WILL SHOW YOU.

KIM LED THE LAMA INTO THE MUSEUM.

YONDER IS THE SAHIB WHO RUNS THE WONDER HOUSE.

THE CURATOR OF THE MUSEUM APPROACHED THE OLD MAN.

WELCOME, O LAMA. COME TO MY OFFICE AWHILE. I WOULD HEAR NEWS OF YOUR COUNTRY.

THE CURATOR LED THE LAMA TO A WOODEN CUBICLE. KIM SAT HIMSELF DOWN, HIS EAR AGAINST A CRACK, TO LISTEN.

THE TALK WAS OF RELIGION AND HOLY PLACES. THEN...

AS A PILGRIM TO THE HOLY PLACES, I ACQUIRE MERIT. BUT THERE IS MORE TO BE DONE.

WHEN OUR GRACOIUS LORD BUDDHA WAS A YOUTH, HE SHOT AN ARROW THAT PASSED BEYOND SIGHT. IT FELL, AND WHERE IT TOUCHED THE EARTH, THERE BROKE OUT A RIVER. IT IS WRITTEN THAT HE WHO BATHES IN THE RIVER WASHES AWAY ALL TAINT OF SIN.

A DREAM TOLD ME TO FIND THE RIVER OF THE ARROW. SO I CAME. BUT WHERE IS THE RIVER?

ALAS, MY BROTHER, I DO NOT KNOW.

I GO TO FIND IT. FAREWELL.

THE LAMA LEFT THE MUSEUM, KIM FOLLOWING LIKE A SHADOW.

WHAT DOST THOU DO NOW?

I GO TO BENARES. BUT IT IS LONG SINCE I HAVE EATEN.

GIVE ME THY BEGGING BOWL. I KNOW THE PEOPLE OF THIS CITY. I WILL BRING IT BACK FILLED.

KIM TROTTED OFF TO THE SHOP OF A VEGETABLE SELLER HE KNEW.

O MY MOTHER, FILL ME THIS BOWL. THERE IS A NEW PRIEST IN THE CITY, AND HE WAITS.

GRUMBLING, THE WOMAN COMPLIED.

THY BOWL IS BIGGER THAN THY HEAD.

KIM RAN BACK TO THE LAMA.

THUS DO WE BEG WHO KNOW THE WAY OF IT. EAT NOW, AND I WILL EAT WITH THEE.

THEY ATE TOGETHER IN GREAT CONTENT. THEN...

I THINK THOU ART SENT TO ME TO BE MY DISCIPLE, EVEN, PERHAPS, TO LEAD ME TO THE RIVER OF THE ARROW.

I WILL GO WITH THEE, AS I HAVE NEVER SEEN ANYONE LIKE THEE IN ALL MY LIFE. BUT I KNOW NOT WHERE THE RIVER IS.

I, TOO, LOOK FOR SOMETHING. MY FATHER SAID THAT SOME DAY THERE WILL COME FOR ME A RED BULL ON A GREEN FIELD WHO SHALL HELP ME.

TO WHAT, CHILD?

GOD KNOWS, BUT MY FATHER TOLD ME. I, TOO, MUST GO A-TRAVELING. IF IT IS OUR FATE TO FIND THOSE THINGS, WE SHALL FIND THEM--THOU THY RIVER, AND I MY BULL.

THEN LET US GO TO BENARES.

NOT BY NIGHT. THIEVES ARE ABROAD. COME WITH ME TO THE SQUARE WHERE THE HORSE CARAVANS PUT UP. I HAVE A FRIEND THERE. WE SHALL GET GOOD LODGING FOR THE NIGHT.

THE BAZAARS BLAZED WITH LIGHT AS THEY MADE THEIR WAY THROUGH THE CROWDED STREETS.

FINALLY THEY REACHED THE SQUARE.

WHOM DO WE SEEK?

A HORSE-TRADER, MAHBUB ALI. I DO LITTLE ERRANDS FOR HIM SOMETIMES.

MAHBUB ALI!

LITTLE FRIEND OF ALL THE WORLD, WHAT IS THIS?

I AM NOW THIS HOLY MAN'S DISCIPLE, AND WE GO TO BENARES. I AM TIRED OF LAHORE. I WISH NEW AIR AND WATER.

WHY COME TO ME?

TO WHOM ELSE SHOULD I COME? I HAVE NO MONEY. IT IS NOT GOOD TO GO ABOUT WITHOUT MONEY.

UMBALLA IS ON THE WAY TO BENARES. CARRY A MESSAGE THERE FROM ME, AND I WILL GIVE THEE MONEY.

GO TO THE ENGLISH OFFICER, COLONEL CREIGHTON, AND SAY THAT THE PEDIGREE OF THE WHITE STALLION I SOLD HIM IS FULLY ESTABLISHED. BUT SPEAK IT TO NO ONE ELSE.

A SHADOW PASSED BEHIND KIM AND MAHBUB ALI SPOKE LOUDLY.

ALLAH! ART THOU THE ONLY BEGGAR IN THE CITY?

HE TOSSED KIM A PIECE OF SOFT, GREASY BREAD.

GO WITH THE LAMA AND LIE DOWN AMONG MY HORSE BOYS FOR TONIGHT

KIM SLUNK AWAY, HIS TEETH IN THE BREAD AND, AS HE EXPECTED, HE FOUND IN IT A SMALL WAD OF PAPER AND THREE SILVER COINS.

HE PAYS WELL. I DO NOT THINK THIS ERRAND CONCERNS ONLY A WHITE STALLION.

DURING THE NIGHT, MAHBUB ALI LEFT HIS STALL. SHORTLY BEFORE DAWN, KIM HEARD FOOTSTEPS.

WHO ENTERS MAHBUB ALI'S STALL?

HE PUT ONE EYE AGAINST A KNOT-HOLE.

HE SEARCHES FOR SOMETHING. IT MUST BE THE PAPER I CARRY TO UMBALLA.

THOSE WHO SEARCH BAGS WITH KNIVES MAY PRESENTLY SEARCH BELLIES WITH KNIVES. IT IS TIME TO GO.

HE WOKE THE SLEEPING LAMA. THEY LEFT THE SQUARE AND BOARDED A TRAIN, BUT AFTER SEVERAL HOURS.

THE SPEED AND CLATTER IRK ME. MOREOVER, I THINK THAT MAYBE WE HAVE OVERPASSED THE RIVER.

WE WILL GET OFF AT UMBALLA AND, IF IT PLEASE THEE, WE WILL HUNT THY RIVER ON FOOT, SO THAT WE MISS NOTHING.

BUT THOU HAST A SEARCH OF THINE OWN. A RED BULL ON A GREEN FIELD, WAS IT NOT?

AY. SO MY FATHER TOLD ME.

AT LAST THEY REACHED UMBALLA.

I GO FOR AWHILE. DO NOT STRAY TILL I RETURN.

KIM SOUGHT OUT THE HOUSE OF THE ENGLISH OFFICER, COLONEL CREIGHTON.

AS HE CROUCHED IN THE SHADOWS, THE COLONEL CAME OUT.

PROTECTOR OF THE POOR! MAHBUB ALI SAYS THAT THE PEDIGREE OF THE WHITE STALLION IS FULLY ESTABLISHED.

WHAT PROOF IS THERE?

THIS!

THE WAD OF PAPER LANDED AT THE COLONEL'S FEET.

HE PICKED IT UP SWIFTLY AND STRODE INTO THE HOUSE.

KIM WORMED HIS WAY NEARER.

HE IS STUDYING THE MESSAGE.

JUST THEN A LANDAU PULLED UP. A TALL MAN GOT OUT AND WAS GREETED BY THE COLONEL.

WOULD YOU COME WITH ME FOR A FEW MINUTES, SIR? I WOULD LIKE YOUR ADVICE ABOUT A WHITE STALLION.

THE TWO MEN WENT IN.

THIS JUST ARRIVED.

I'VE BEEN EXPECTING IT FOR SOME TIME.

THEN IT MEANS WAR?

NO. LET'S CALL IT PUNISHMENT. FIVE NATIVE KINGS ARE PREPARING AN UPRISING. WE WILL STRIKE THEM BEFORE THEY ARE READY. CALL UP TWO BRIGADES IMMEDIATELY. EIGHT THOUSAND MEN SHOULD BE ENOUGH.

THE MEN PASSED INTO ANOTHER PART OF THE HOUSE.

I MUST FIND OUT WHO THE OTHER SAHIB IS.

KIM CRAWLED AROUND TO THE KITCHEN.

I CAME TO WASH DISHES IN RETURN FOR DINNER.

THINK YOU THAT WE WHO SERVE CREIGHTON SAHIB NEED STRANGE BOYS TO HELP US WHEN HE ENTERTAINS THE COMMANDER-IN-CHIEF? BEGONE!

KIM SCURRIED AWAY.

HO, SO THE TALL ONE IS THE COMMANDER-IN-CHIEF. HE WILL LOOSE A GREAT ARMY TO PUNISH SOMEONE! THIS IS BIG NEWS!

WHEN HE REACHED THE PLACE WHERE THE LAMA WAS, HE FOUND HIM TALKING TO AN ASTROLOGER.

THIS IS A HOLY MAN. HIS METHODS ARE WISE AND SURE.

TELL ME, THEN--WILL I FIND MY RED BULL ON A GREEN FIELD?

WHEN WAST THOU BORN?

THE FIRST NIGHT OF MAY, THE YEAR OF THE EARTHQUAKE IN SRINAGUR.

THE ASTROLOGER MADE SOME SCRATCHES IN THE DUST. THEN...

THUS SAY THE STARS. WITHIN THREE DAYS COME TWO MEN TO MAKE THINGS READY. AFTER THEM FOLLOWS THE BULL, BUT THE SIGN OVER HIM IS THE SIGN OF WAR AND ARMED MEN.

TELL ME, WHY SHOULD ONE WHOSE STAR LEADS HIM TO WAR FOLLOW A HOLY

BECAUSE I HAVE NEVER SEEN ONE TRULY HOLY IN TALK AND IN ACT AS THIS LAMA.

THE NEXT DAY, THEY SET OUT ON THEIR SEARCH FOR THE RIVER AND THE BULL. THEY WALKED ALL THAT DAY AND THE NEXT. TOWARD NIGHTFALL ON THE SECOND DAY, THEY CAME TO A RESTING PLACE WHERE KIM FELL INTO CONVERSATION WITH A WEALTHY OLD WIDOW.

CAN THE HOLY ONE YOU TRAVEL WITH MAKE A PRAYER SO THAT MY DAUGHTER WILL HAVE A SECOND SON?

HE HAS GREAT POWERS. I WILL ASK HIM TO SPEAK TO THEE.

THE LAMA TALKED TO THE WOMAN. WHEN HE RETURNED TO KIM...

SHE JOURNEYS TO THE SOUTH, AS WE DO. SHE GREATLY DESIRES THAT WE JOURNEY WITH HER.

GOOD. SHE IS RICH AND WILL CARE FOR US WELL.

DID YOU FORSEE THIS, LITTLE FRIEND?

I DESIRE ONLY TO OVERSEE YOUR COMFORTS, HOLY ONE.

A BLESSING ON THEE. I HAVE KNOWN MANY MEN, BUT TO NONE HAS MY HEART GONE OUT AS IT HAS TO THEE.

THEY TRAVELLED THE NEXT DAY WITH THE WIDOW'S CARAVAN. BEFORE SUNDOWN, THEY MADE CAMP. KIM AND THE LAMA WALKED IDLY ACROSS THE COUNTRYSIDE.

LOOK, SOLDIERS COME OUR WAY.

KEEP BEHIND THIS TREE!

OFFICERS' TENTS HERE, I SUPPOSE. AND THE BAGGAGE-WAGGONS BEHIND?

I THINK THEY ARE MARKING OUT A CAMP.

AFTER SOME DISCUSSION, THE SOLDIERS STUCK THEIR MARKERS AND WALKED AWAY.

O, HOLY ONE, MY PROPHECY! REMEMBER-- FIRST COME TWO TO MAKE THINGS READY, AND AFTER THEM COMES THE RED BULL ON THE GREEN FIELD.

LOOK! THERE IT IS!

NOT TEN FEET AWAY, A MARKING FLAG BEARING A REGIMENTAL INSIGNIA WHIPPED IN THE BREEZE.

CERTAINLY IT IS THY BULL. AND CERTAINLY THE TWO MEN CAME TO MAKE ALL READY. WHAT IS TO HAPPEN NOW?.

HARK, THE SOLDIERS APPROACH.

THEY WATCHED FROM THEIR HIDING PLACE AS THE REGIMENT ARRIVED AND QUICKLY MADE CAMP.

LET US GO BACK NOW, AND COME BACK WHEN IT IS DARK.

WHEN EVENING FELL, KIM AND THE LAMA AGAIN APPROACHED THE CAMP.

WAIT HERE TILL I CALL. I MUST CREEP CLOSER AND SEE MORE OF MY BULL.

KIM WRIGGLED TO THE DOOR OF THE MESS TENT.

THERE IS THE BULL. I THINK THEY PRAY TO IT.

SO ABSORBED WAS KIM THAT HE DID NOT SEE THE CHAPLAIN OF THE REGIMENT RISE TO LEAVE.

THEN...

AS THE CHAPLAIN FELL, HE GRABBED KIM AND HELD ON.

HE HAULED THE STRUGGLING BOY TO HIS TENT.

ARE YOU A THIEF?

NO! NO!

IN THE STRUGGLE, THE STRING TO AN AMULET CASE KIM WORE ABOUT HIS NECK SNAPPED.

WHAT IS THIS?

IT IS MY PAPERS! OH, DO NOT TAKE THEM. MY FATHER TOLD ME ALWAYS TO WEAR THEM.

THE CHAPLAIN TOOK NO HEED, BUT, GOING TO THE TENT DOOR, CALLED ALOUD.

I WANT YOUR ADVICE, FATHER VICTOR. HERE IS A HINDU BOY WHO TALKS ENGLISH AND VALUES SOME SORT OF CHARM AROUND HIS NECK.

ANOTHER CHAPLAIN ENTERED. THEY OPENED KIM'S AMULET AND FOUND HIS BIRTH CERTIFICATE AND TWO REGIMENTAL PAPERS WHICH HAD BELONGED TO HIS FATHER.

POWERS OF DARKNESS BELOW! THIS IS KIMBALL O'HARA'S SON. IS IT POSSIBLE?

WHAT IS YOUR NAME?

KIM.

TELL ME ABOUT YOURSELF, KIM.

MY FATHER AND MOTHER ARE DEAD SINCE I WAS VERY LITTLE. I AM AT PRESENT THE DISCIPLE OF A VERY HOLY MAN WHO WAITS FOR ME OUTSIDE.

I WILL SEND FOR HIM.

DIGNIFIED AND UNSUSPICIOUS, THE LAMA STRODE INTO THE TENT.

I HAVE FOUND THE BULL, BUT GOD KNOWS WHAT COMES NEXT.

IT WILL BE BEST IF WE KEEP THIS BOY AND PUT HIM IN A SCHOOL WHERE HE WILL HAVE PROPER CARE.

BUT HE IS MY DISCIPLE, WE TRAVEL TOGETHER IN SEARCH OF A RIVER.

HE IS A SOLDIER'S SON. HE HAS MIRACULOUSLY FOUND HIS FATHER'S REGIMENT. WE WILL NOW TAKE CARE OF HIM.

THE LAMA TURNED SADLY TO KIM.

MY HEART WENT OUT TO THEE. NOW THEY TAKE THEE FROM ME. WOE!

I WILL NOT STAY. I WILL RUN AWAY AND RETURN TO THEE.

NO, THOU ART A SAHIB AND SHOULD BE BROUGHT UP MAS A SAHIB. BUT I MUST KNOW HOW THEY WILL TEACH THEE.

THERE IS THE MILITARY ORPHANAGE OR THE MASONIC SCHOOL. OF COURSE, ST. XAVIER'S IN LUCKNOW IS THE BEST SCHOOL IN INDIA, BUT...

HOW MUCH MONEY FOR IT?

TWO OR THREE HUNDRED RUPEES A YEAR.

WRITE THE NAME OF THE SCHOOL UPON A PAPER. THY NAME, ALSO. I WILL SEND THEE MONEY FOR THIS SCHOOL.

BUT HOW WOULD YOU GET IT?

IN TIBET I HAVE HONOUR. I ASK FOR WHAT I NEED, AND THEY SEND IT.

NOW I GO TO FOLLOW MY SEARCH. FAREWELL, LITTLE FRIEND.

STAY WITH THE RICH WIDOW. SHE WILL FEED THEE UNTIL I RUN BACK TO THEE.

KIM WAS TURNED OVER TO A SERGEANT.

HAVE A CARE HE DOESN'T SLIP THROUGH YOUR FINGERS BEFORE WE GET TO SANAWAR.

YOU WILL NOT GO TO SANAWAR. YOU WILL GO TO THE WAR.

WHAT WAR? ARE YOU A PROPHET?

I TELL YOU THAT WHEN YOU GET TO UMBALLA, YOU WILL BE SENT TO THE WAR. IT IS A WAR OF 8,000 MEN.

TAKE HIM AWAY, SERGEANT. WHO SAYS THE AGE OF MIRACLES IS GONE BY? MY POOR MIND HAS HAD ENOUGH FOR ONE NIGHT.

THE NEXT MORNING THE REGIMENT TOOK THE ROAD TO UMBALLA. BUT BEFORE LONG, NEW ORDERS CAME.

WE ARE TO GO TO THE WAR TOMORROW. NOW, MY SON, HOW DID YOU KNOW?

NO MATTER. BUT NOW WILL YOU LET ME GO BACK TO MY OLD MAN? I AM AFRAID HE WILL DIE WITHOUT ME.

NO. WE'LL KEEP YOU AND MAKE A MAN OF YOU.

THE NEXT DAY, THE REGIMENT ENTRAINED FOR THE FRONT. KIM WAS LEFT BEHIND WITH THE SICK, THE WIVES, AND THE BOYS.

HERE, YOU! WHERE ARE YOU GOING? MY ORDERS ARE NOT TO LET YOU OUT OF MY SIGHT.

JUST DOWN THE ROAD.

ALL RIGHT. BUT DON'T TRY TO RUN AWAY-- THE PICKETS WILL LEAD YOU BACK QUICKER THAN YOU STARTED OUT.

KIM WENT TO A TREE NEAR THE ROAD AND EYED THE NATIVES AS THEY PASSED. SOON...

YOU--GO TO THE NEAREST LETTER-WRITER AND TELL HIM TO COME HERE AT ONCE.

THE NATIVE SHUFFLED OFF, AND SOON A LETTER-WRITER APPEARED.

I WOULD WRITE A LETTER TO MAHBUB ALI, THE HORSE-TRADER. BEGIN, "I CARRIED THE NEWS OF THE STALLION'S PEDIGREE TO UMBALLA.

"BUT THEN I FOUND THE REGIMENT OF THE RED BULL AND WAS CAUGHT. I DO NOT LIKE IT HERE. COME THEN, AND HELP ME."

THE LETTER DISPATCHED, KIM RETURNED TO THE BARRACKS. SOON HE WAS CALLED BEFORE FATHER VICTOR.

I'VE HEARD FROM YOUR FRIEND, THE LAMA.

WHERE IS HE? IS HE WELL?

YOU ARE FOND OF HIM, THEN?

OH, YES. AND HE WAS FOND OF ME.

IT SEEMS SO. HE SAYS HE IS SENDING THREE HUNDRED RUPEES A YEAR SO THAT YOU CAN GO TO ST. XAVIER'S. WE'LL SEND YOU UP IN A WEEK OR SO.

FOR THE NEXT THREE DAYS, KIM ENDURED THE HATED, ORDERLY LIFE OF THE BARRACKS. THEN, ON THE MORNING OF THE FOURTH DAY...

MAHBUB ALI!

THE HORSE-TRADER SWEPT HIM UP TO THE SADDLE.

OH, TAKE ME AWAY FROM HERE!

HOW CAN I? THEY WOULD PUT ME IN JAIL.

BE PATIENT. WHEN THOU ART A MAN--WHO KNOWS--THOU WILT BE GRATEFUL TO HAVE FOUND THINE OWN PEOPLE.

JUST THEN, AN ENGLISHMAN RACED ALONGSIDE.

HI, MAHBUB, PULL UP!

IT IS THE ONE I DELIVERED THE MESSAGE TO!

WHAT THE DEUCE HAVE YOU GOT THERE?

A BOY, I TAKE HIM FOR A RIDE.

HE HAS MANY TALENTS. HE DELIVERED A MESSAGE FOR ME ONCE ABOUT A WHITE STALLION.

AH, AND WHERE DO YOU TAKE HIM?

BACK TO THE REGIMENT THAT FOUND HIM.

THEY RODE UP TO THE BARRACKS.

GOOD MORNING. THIS BOY OF YOURS SEEMS RATHER A CURIOSITY.

THAT HE IS. IF YOU HAVE A FEW MINUTES, I'LL TELL YOU ABOUT HIM. PERHAPS YOU CAN ADVISE ME.

CREIGHTON AND THE CHAPLAIN WENT OFF, LEAVING KIM AND MAHBUB ALI ALONE.

AND I THOUGHT YOU WOULD HELP ME!

BELIEVE ME, LITTLE FRIEND OF ALL THE WORLD, I DO THEE A SERVICE. THROUGH ME THE COLONEL SAHIB MAY RAISE THEE TO HONOUR.

NAY. I WANT ONLY TO TAKE TO THE ROAD AND FIND MY LAMA AGAIN.

SOON THE COLONEL RETURNED.

I'VE ARRANGED TO LOOK AFTER YOU ON THE TRIP TO ST. XAVIER'S. THEREFORE, SIT STILL FOR THREE DAYS, AND WE WILL MEET AGAIN.

AS THE COLONEL LEFT...

AS REGARDS THE YOUNG HORSE, I SAY THAT WHEN A COLT IS BORN TO BE A POLO PONY, IT IS A GREAT WRONG TO BREAK THAT COLT TO A HEAVY CART.

SO DO I, MAHBUB. THE COLT WILL BE ENTERED FOR POLO ONLY.

THREE DAYS LATER, KIM WAS ON THE TRAIN TO LUCKNOW WITH THE COLONEL.

YOU WILL LEARN HOW TO BE A SURVEYOR AT ST. XAVIER'S. IF YOU WORK HARD, I WILL SEE THAT YOU FIND SUITABLE EMPLOYMENT WHEN YOU ARE FINISHED WITH SCHOOL.

YOU MUST LEARN HOW TO MAKE PICTURES OF ROADS AND MOUNTAINS AND RIVERS--TO CARRY THESE PICTURES IN YOUR EYE TILL A SUITABLE TIME COMES TO SET THEM ON PAPER.

HE WILL USE ME AS MAHBUB ALI DID, I THINK.

TWENTY-FOUR HOURS LATER, THEY ARRIVED AT LUCKNOW.

WE SHALL MEET AGAIN, IF YOU ARE OF GOOD SPIRIT. BUT YOU ARE NOT YET TRIED.

NOT EVEN WHEN I BROUGHT YOU THE STALLION'S PEDIGREE?

MUCH IS GAINED BY FORGETTING, LITTLE BROTHER. FAREWELL.

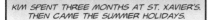

KIM SPENT THREE MONTHS AT ST. XAVIER'S. THEN CAME THE SUMMER HOLIDAYS.

THE SCHOOL IS CLOSED FROM AUGUST TO OCTOBER. I HAVE BEEN INSTRUCTED TO SEND YOU TO A BARRACK-SCHOOL NEAR UMBALLA FOR THAT TIME.

THAT NIGHT...

MY HOLIDAY IS MINE-- TO DO WITH AS I PLEASE.

KIM MADE HIS WAY TO A CERTAIN SHOP.

WHAT DOST THOU WANT?

A LITTLE DYE-STUFF AND THREE YARDS OF CLOTH.

AN HOUR LATER HE EMERGED-- A LOW-CASTE HINDU BOY.

AH, WHAT FAT DAYS ARE AHEAD! IF I ONLY KNEW WHERE MY LAMA WAS!

KIM SPENT TWO PERFECT MONTHS ROAMING AROUND INDIA. THEN ONE DAY...

MAHBUB ALI!!

OHO! WHERE HAST THOU BEEN?

UP AND DOWN-- DOWN AND UP.

I HAVE A MESSAGE FROM CREIGHTON SAHIB. THOU ART TO LODGE IN LURGAN SAHIB'S HOUSE TILL IT IS TIME TO GO AGAIN TO ST. XAVIER'S.

I HAD SOONER LODGE WITH THEE. WHO IS THIS LURGAN?

HE HAS A JEWELRY SHOP AMONG THE EUROPEAN SHOPS IN SIMLA. GO AND FIND HIM. HE HAS MUCH TO TEACH YOU. HERE BEGINS THE GREAT GAME.

AT LURGAN'S SHOP, KIM WAS TAUGHT MANY CURIOUS GAMES.

LOOK AT THESE JEWELS CAREFULLY. THEN I WILL COVER THEM AND YOU MUST NAME AND DESCRIBE THEM EXACTLY.

IN THE AFTERNOONS, KIM WOULD SIT HIDDEN BEHIND A SCREEN WATCHING THE MANY PEOPLE WHO CAME TO THE SHOP. IN THE EVENINGS...

NOW DESCRIBE FOR ME THOSE WHO CAME TODAY.

FREQUENTLY KIM WOULD PLAY AT DRESSING UP.

WELL DONE, O'HARA. I THINK THERE IS A GREAT DEAL IN YOU. SOME DAY YOU WILL BE READY TO PLAY IN THE GREAT GAME.

THEN LURGAN SPOKE OF THE GREAT GAME--THE BRITISH SECRET SERVICE.

FROM TIME TO TIME, GOD CAUSES MEN TO BE BORN WHO HAVE A LUST TO GO ABROAD AND DISCOVER NEWS AT THE RISK OF THEIR LIVES. YOU ARE ONE OF THEM.

TRUE. BUT THE DAYS GO SLOWLY FOR ME. I AM YET A BOY.

HAVE PATIENCE, FRIEND OF ALL THE WORLD. GO BACK TO SCHOOL AND STUDY HARD. MAKE YOURSELF READY FOR THE GREAT GAME.

KIM WENT BACK TO SCHOOL, ACCOMPANIED BY A FRIEND OF LURGAN'S, HUREE BABU.

WHEN YOUR STUDIES ARE ENDED, I HOPE SOME DAY TO ENJOY YOUR OFFICIAL AQUAINTANCE.

AT ST. XAVIER'S, KIM EXCELLED IN MATHEMATICS AND MAP-MAKING. ONCE HE WAS ABLE TO SEE THE LAMA.

CAN I NOT GO WITH THEE?

THE TIME HAS NOT YET COME. FIRST THOU MUST GET ALL THE WISDOM OF THE SAHIBS.

THEN ONE DAY IN KIM'S THIRD YEAR, COLONEL CREIGHTON AND MAHBUB ALI MET IN LURGAN'S SHOP.

THE PONY IS MADE-- FINISHED, SAHIB. LOOSE THE REIN AND LET HIM GO. WE NEED HIM.

BUT HE IS SO YOUNG--NOT MORE THAN SIXTEEN.

HE NEEDN'T CARRY A HEAVY LOAD AT FIRST. LET HIM GO OUT WITH HIS LAMA FOR SIX MONTHS. HE WILL GET EXPERIENCE AND KNOWLEDGE.

ALL RIGHT. HUREE BABU CAN WATCH OVER THEM.

I AM LOOSED FROM THE SCHOOL. I CAME TO THEE.

SO! THOU ART NO LONGER A CHILD, BUT A MAN, RIPENED IN WISDOM.

MY TEACHING I OWE TO THEE. FOR THREE YEARS I HAVE EATEN THY BREAD.

I DID WELL. NOW WE TAKE THE ROAD AND OUR SEARCH. WITH THEE, I SHALL FIND MY RIVER. WE ARE TOGETHER AGAIN, FRIEND OF ALL THE WORLD.

THE NEXT MORNING, THEY STARTED OUT.

LET US GO NORTH. I REMEMBER A PLEASANT PLACE BY SAHARUNPORE.

THAT IS WHERE THE RICH WIDOW LIVES--THE ONE I LEFT THEE WITH WHEN THE ARMY TOOK ME AWAY.

THEY TRAVELLED TO SAHARUNPORE, WHERE THE WIDOW GREETED THEM.

THOU ART WELCOME. A ROOM AND FOOD AWAIT YE.

MAYBE THOU WILT GIVE ME A CHARM FOR MY GRANDSON'S COLICS? I TRUST IT SOONER THAN THE HAKIM'S MEDICINE.

WHO IS THE HAKIM?

A WANDERING MASTER OF MEDICINE. HE HAS BEEN HERE FOUR DAYS. NOW HEARING YE WERE COMING, HE HAS GONE TO COVER.

AFTER ALL BUT KIM HAD RETIRED, THE HAKIM APPEARED.

MY MEDICINES ARE SURER THAN THE CHARMS OF THY HOLY ONE.

WHAT DRUGS HAST THOU?

NONE BUT THE BEST, MR. O'HARA! I AM JOLLY GLAD TO SEE YOU AGAIN.

HUREE BABU! I WOULD NOT HAVE KNOWN YOU! WHY ARE YOU HERE?

I HEARD YOU AND THE LAMA WERE HEADED THIS WAY AND CAME UP TO SEE YOU.

BUT WHY? IS IT THE GREAT GAME? I WANT TO HELP.

WELL, IT IS KNOWN THAT TWO STRANGERS HAVE COME DOWN FROM THE MOUNTAINS OF THE NORTH UNDER COVER OF SHOOTING WILD GOATS. THEY HAVE GUNS, BUT THEY ALSO HAVE CHAINS AND LEVELS AND COMPASSES.

UP THE VALLEY, DOWN THE VALLEY, THEY GO, MAKING OBSERVATIONS.

FOR?

FOR THE RUSSIANS. SO I HAVE BEEN ORDERED TO GO NORTH AND WATCH THE STRANGERS.

BUT WHAT CAN I DO?

PERSUADE YOUR OLD MAN TO TRAVEL NORTH ALSO, SO THAT YOU CAN BE READY TO ASSIST ME IN AN EMERGENCY.

HUREE BABU SET OUT FOR THE NORTH THE NEXT DAY. KIM AND THE LAMA FOLLOWED SEVERAL MILES BEHIND.

FEEL THE COOL AIR FROM TIBET! IT BLOWS AWAY TWENTY YEARS FROM THE LIFE OF A MAN.

DAY AFTER DAY, THEY STRUCK DEEPER INTO THE MOUNTAINS. AHEAD OF THEM, HUREE BABU SEARCHED UNTIL HE SPOTTED THE TENTS OF THE RUSSIANS.

HE APPEARED BEFORE THEM IN A RAINSTORM.

I AM AGENT FOR THE RAJAH OF RAMPUR, GENTLEMEN. WHAT CAN I DO FOR YOU, PLEASE?

DELIGHTED TO SEE YOU. CAN YOU GET THESE HILLMEN TO PICK UP OUR BASKETS AGAIN SO THAT WE MAY PROCEED? THE RAINSTORM HAS FRIGHTENED THEM.

INDEED--ARE THESE THE BASKETS?

HE UPSET A BASKET WITH A RED OILSKIN TOP.

OH, FORGIVE ME. I AM CLUMSY.

HUREE BABU TOSSED THE HILLMEN SOME SILVER. THEY PICKED UP THE BASKETS AND THE RUSSIANS RESUMED THEIR JOURNEY. ON THE SECOND DAY, AT SUNSET, THEY MET KIM AND THE LAMA.

AND WHO IS THIS?

AN EMINENT HOLY MAN. HE IS EXPLAINING A HOLY PICTURE TO HIS DISCIPLE.

THAT IS CURIOUS. LET US LISTEN A MOMENT.

AS THE RUSSIANS WATCHED THE LAMA...

THESE ARE THE MEN. ALL THEIR REPORTS AND MAPS ARE IN THE BASKET WITH THE RED TOP.

WHAT CAN I DO?

WAIT AND SEE. IF ANY CHANCE COMES, YOU WILL KNOW WHERE TO SEEK FOR THE PAPERS.

THEN...

THAT IS ENOUGH. I CANNOT UNDERSTAND HIM, BUT I WANT THE PICTURE.

HE WOULD NOT SELL IT-- IT IS VERY HOLY.

OH, COME! NOW LET'S NOT HAGGLE OVER IT.

THE LAMA ROSE ANGRILY.

YOU HAVE DEFILED THE HOLY WORD!

THE RUSSIAN STRUCK THE OLD MAN FULL IN THE FACE.

THE NEXT INSTANT, KIM WAS AT HIS THROAT.

THE HILLMEN SCATTERED IN FRIGHT, PULLING THE LAMA ALONG WITH THEM.

DON'T SHOOT, SIR. I GO TO THE RESCUE.

GO BACK TO THE HILLMEN. THEY HAVE THE BAGGAGE. GET THE PAPERS FROM THE RED-TOPPED BASKET. GO!

KIM TORE UP THE HILL.

ART THOU HURT, HOLY ONE?

MY HEAD BEATS. COME, WE GO WITH THESE FOLK TO THEIR VILLAGE.

WHEN THEY REACHED THE VILLAGE, THE LAMA WAS PUT TO BED. THEN...

THOU HAST THE BAGGAGE?

YES, BUT THERE IS ONE BASKET WHOSE NATURE WE DO NOT KNOW.

BUT I DO. IT IS FULL OF WONDERFUL THINGS, NOT TO BE HANDLED BY FOOLS.

WILL IT BETRAY US?

NOT IF IT IS GIVEN TO ME. I WILL DRAW OUT ITS MAGIC.

HERE, THEN. THERE IS MORE THAN ENOUGH FOR ALL OF US.

KIM EMPTIED THE BASKET.

MAPS, LETTERS-- IT IS A FINE HAUL!

HE PUT THE DOCUMENTS INSIDE HIS ROBE.

I MUST TELL HUREE BABU WHAT HAS HAPPENED, AND ASK HIM WHAT I AM TO DO NEXT. BUT HE MUST STILL BE WITH THE RUSSIANS.

JUST THEN A WOMAN ENTERED.

WILT THOU CARRY A MESSAGE FOR ME TO THE BABU WHO GOES WITH THE RUSSIANS?

YES.

KIM SCRIBBLED A NOTE.

I have everything. tell me what to do. ——

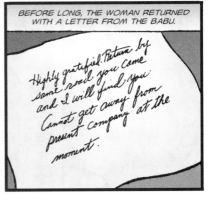

BEFORE LONG, THE WOMAN RETURNED WITH A LETTER FROM THE BABU.

Highly gratified. Return by same road you came and I will find you. Cannot get away from present company at the moment.

SUPPORTING THE LAMA, KIM STARTED DOWN THE MOUNTAIN.

THOU ART ILL. LET US REST FOR AWHILE.

NAY, THE TIME IS SHORT, AND MY SEARCH IS NOT FINISHED.

THEY TRAVELLED SLOWLY, KIM STAGGERING BENEATH THE BURDEN OF THE OLD MAN.

NEVER WAS THERE, FRIEND OF ALL THE WORLD, A MORE FAITHFUL DISCIPLE THAN THEE. BUT I STEAL THY STRENGTH. THOU ART WEAKENED.

TELL ME, HAST THOU NEVER A WISH TO LEAVE ME?

I AM NOT A DOG OR A SNAKE TO BITE WHEN I HAVE LEARNED TO LOVE.

FINALLY, AFTER MANY WEARY MILES, THEY REACHED SAHARUNPORE AND THE WIDOW'S HOUSE.

HE HAS A SICKNESS, FOR I HAVE LIVED UPON HIS STRENGTH.

WE MUST RESTORE HIM.

KIM WAS PUT TO BED.

HAST THOU A LOCKED BOX IN WHICH TO KEEP HOLY BOOKS?

IT SHALL BE BROUGHT.

KIM LOCKED AWAY THE RUSSIAN'S PAPERS WITH A GROAN OF RELIEF.

HE FELL INTO A STUPOR, AFTER MANY DAYS, HE AWAKENED.

WHERE IS MY HOLY ONE?

HE IS WELL, THOUGH THAT IS NONE OF *HIS* DOING.

HE ROVED THE FIELDS FOR TWO NIGHTS ON AN EMPTY BELLY AND THEN TUMBLED INTO A BROOK. HE MIGHT HAVE DROWNED, BUT THE HAKIM FISHED HIM OUT.

THE HAKIM IS HERE?

HE CAME A FEW DAYS AGO. HE IS FULL OF ANXIETY FOR THY HEALTH.

SEND HIM HERE, MOTHER.

THE WIDOW LEFT. SOON HUREE BABU ENTERED.

BY JOVE, I AM GLAD TO SEE YOU.

THE PAPERS ARE IN THE BOX. HERE IS THE KEY.

THE BABU EMPTIED THE BOX EAGERLY.

THIS IS FINE! THE BRITISH GOVERNMENT WILL BE DELIGHTED TO GET THEM. YOU DID WELL!

WHERE ARE THE RUSSIANS?

AS THEIR GREAT GAME COLLAPSED, THEY WENT BACK TO THEIR OWN COUNTRY IN DISGRACE.

THAT IS GOOD. BUT NOW I AM SO SLEEPY.

KIM SLEPT. TOWARD EVENING, THE LAMA CAME WITH MAHBUB ALI, THE HORSE-TRADER.

I AM CLEANSED AND FREE OF SIN, AND HE SHALL BE ALSO. THEN HE SHALL GO FORTH AS A TEACHER.

BUT HE IS URGENTLY NEEDED BY THE STATE.

TO THAT END, HE WAS PREPARED. HE AIMED ME IN MY SEARCH, I AIDED HIM IN HIS. LET HIM WORK FOR THE STATE. IT DOES NOT MATTER.

MAHBUB ALI LEFT. THEN KIM AWOKE.

HOLY ONE! ART THOU WELL?

YES, AND I BRING THEE NEWS. THE SEARCH IS FINISHED!

WHEN WE RETURNED HERE I TOOK NO FOOD, I DRANK NO WATER FOR TWO DAYS AND NIGHTS. MY SOUL WENT FREE AS AN EAGLE. I SAW THE RIVER OF THE ARROW AT MY FEET AND, DESCENDING, THE WATERS OF IT CLOSED OVER ME. AND BEHOLD, I WAS FREE FROM SIN, AND THOU SHALT BE, ALSO.

AND THE LAMA SMILED, AS A MAN MAY WHO HAS WON SALVATION FOR HIMSELF AND HIS BELOVED.

THE END

KIM

RUDYARD KIPLING

Pathan horse-traders, Russian spies, and Tibetan holy men; railways and mountains; British Imperial politics and Buddhist philosophy—like the British India that it chronicles and celebrates, Rudyard Kipling's novel *Kim* is a colorful and exciting mixture of many different elements. At first glance *Kim* appears to be only slightly plotted, romping through the exotic Indian landscape after the manner of a picaresque novel (a book which follows the episodic adventures of a *picaro*—the Spanish word for a rogue or adventurer). This apparent looseness of structure, however, hides the fact that *Kim* is actually three stories in one.

On one level *Kim* is what literary critics call a *bildungsroman* (a German term, meaning a story about the protagonist's education and growth from youth into adulthood). We meet Kimball O'Hara—Kim—in his childhood as an irresponsible street youth, and follow him through his education at the hands of a number of unorthodox teachers. At the end of the novel, the roles are reversed, as the young man Kim has become must take responsibility for bringing his ailing mentor Teshoo Lama out of the Himalayan foothills to a place of safety.

Kim is also a novel of espionage, part of a tradition in British popular fiction that includes the works of Ian Fleming, Len Deighton, and John LeCarre—and, in the earlier decades of this century, John Buchan (author of *The Thirty-Nine Steps*). For this aspect of the tale, Kipling deploys all the familiar and well-loved literary devices of the fictional spymaster: beautiful women with loose morals and bad intentions, stolen papers, secret messages, lurking assassins, chases, escapes, and a whole array of impromptu (but effective) disguises.

And finally, *Kim* is a quest novel, the story of the venerable Teshoo Lama's pilgrimage to the holy places of Buddhism, and his search for the River of the Arrow: a miraculous river of legend which sprang up where an arrow shot by the Buddha struck the ground:

> *"And, overshooting all marks,* [the lama said] *the arrow passed far and beyond sight. At the last it fell; and, where it touched earth, there broke out a stream which presently became a River;*

whose nature, by our Lord's beneficence, and that merit he acquired ere He freed himself, is that whoso bathes in it washes away all taint and speckle of sin....By it one obtains freedom from the Wheel of Things."

The book opens as Kim meets Teshoo Lama for the first time and joins the old man on his journey, and it closes with the lama's near-death by drowning in the river at Kula and the completion of his quest:

"I saw the River below me [the lama said]—*the River of the Arrow—and, descending, the waters of it closed over me; and behold I was again in the body of Teshoo Lama, and the hakim [learned man] from Dacca bore up my head in the waters of the River. It is here! It is beyond the mango-tope here—even here!*

THE AUTHOR

Joseph Rudyard Kipling (as a writer, he didn't use his first name) was born in Bombay, India, on December 30, 1865. At the age of six, he was sent away from his family to be educated in England. For British families living in India, this was standard practice. Parents feared the effect of the Indian climate on their children's health, and—perhaps even

more—they feared the effect of Indian culture on their children's character. Sending the children "home" to England was regarded as essential, lest they fail to turn out properly English.

The English household to which the young Kipling was sent may not have been as deliberately cruel as he later painted it in his short story "Baa Baa Black Sheep" and in his unfinished autobiography *Something of Myself*. But to a six-year-old child, the change from the brightly colored, polyglot atmosphere of India, where children were traditionally given a great deal of license, to the "character-building" discipline of Victorian England must have seemed like a transition from heaven to hell. Later, he attended boarding school—United Services College at Westward Ho!, in Devon—before returning to India to work as a journalist.

Kipling grew up, therefore, essentially bilingual and multicultural—that aspect of the character of Kimball O'Hara (the "Kim" of the novel) may have been drawn from his own experience. Kipling was no revolutionary; temperamentally, he remained on the side of those who sought to protect and maintain the existing order of things, rather than of those who sought to change it. Nevertheless, his stories and poems dealt with a far wider range of characters and situations than his identification with British imperialism and the "white man's burden" would at first suggest.

His early training as a writer

came from his time as a journalist back in his beloved India, where from 1882 to 1889 he edited and wrote short stories for the Civil and Military Gazette in the city of Lahore. (It is in Lahore, incidentally, that Kim's adventures in the Great Game, and his travels with Teshoo Lama, have their beginning.) Kipling's first published books were a volume of poetry, *Departmental Ditties*, in 1886, and in 1888 the short story collection, *Plain Tales from the Hills*. Kipling remained primarily a poet and a short story writer all his life, but he also wrote several longer works, of which *Kim*—written in 1896 and first published in 1901—is perhaps the finest example.

Although Kipling's writings are associated in the public mind with the period of British rule in India, he also traveled in America—and tended, in fact, to regard Americans with more sympathy than many Englishmen of the time. He even married an American, Caroline Balestier, in 1892. The Kipling family lived briefly in Vermont before settling permanently in England in 1903.

In 1907 Kipling received the Nobel Prize in literature; he was the first English author to be so honored. He died in London on January 18, 1936.

CHARACTERS

Kim (Kimball O'Hara) The orphaned son of an Irish sergeant in the British army. Kim's early childhood is summed up by Kipling in a few brief sentences:

> *The half-caste-woman who looked after him (she smoked opium, and pretended to keep a second-hand furniture shop by the square where the cheap cabs wait) told the missionaries that she was Kim's mother's sister; but his mother had been nursemaid in a colonel's family and had married Kimball O'Hara, a young colour-sergeant of the Mavericks, an Irish Regiment. He afterwards took a post on the Sind, Punjab, and Delhi railway, and his regiment went home without him. The wife died of cholera in Ferozepore, and O'Hara fell to drink and loafing up and down the line with the keen-eyed three-year-old baby. Societies and chaplains, anxious for the child, tried to catch him, but O'Hara drifted away, till he came across the woman who took opium and learned the taste from her, and died as poor whites do in India.*

One of the many ironies in Kipling's classic novel of the English in India is that its hero, Kim, is not English at all. Kim is Irish—at a time when Ireland, like India, was ruled by England. (Ireland achieved Commonwealth status—a kind of semi-independence under the rule of

the British Crown—in 1922, but full independence did not come until 1949, two years *after* India had celebrated its own independence.) Kim, though he is regarded as a sahib—an Englishman—by his Indian friends, is in fact also the product of an occupied country, someone who is never going to achieve the status of a true Englishman.

Kim's outstanding characteristic is his chameleon-like ability to shift lan-

guages and customs in order to blend in with whatever group he finds himself among. This gift is enhanced by the fact that Kim grew up bilingual— learning English from his soldier father and Hindustani from the woman, apparently his father's mistress, who looked after him following his mother's death. (More than 1600 languages or dialects are spoken in India, comprising 14 major

language groups—it's not really surprising that someone like Kim could blend into the crowd.) To

Mahbub Ali and Creighton Sahib, he is a clever urchin and a potential spy; to the teachers at St. Xavier's school, he is an apt pupil; and to Teshoo Lama, who believes in his innate goodness, he is a loyal and devoted *chela*.

Teshoo Lama An elderly lama (Tibetan Buddhist monk) on a religious pilgrimage to the holy places of the Buddhist faith. He first encounters Kim in the city of Lahore, where the boy—amused by the lama's unworldliness—appoints himself Teshoo Lama's *chela*. In return, after Kim has been "rescued" from life as a street urchin by the chaplains of his father's regiment, the lama pays for his education at St. Xavier's school. Further, he searches on Kim's behalf as well as his own for the River of the Arrow, whose waters

will free those who wash in it from the wheel of reincarnation.

Teshoo Lama resembles Kim in that he is both outside regular Indian society (as a Tibetan foreigner and as a wandering holy man) and a part of it. His role as an outsider allows him to mingle, as Kim does, with representatives of different castes and ethnicities. Like other Buddhist monks and wandering holy men, he supports himself by begging—giving others the chance to "acquire merit," as the phrase goes, by making charitable offerings. Part of Kim's work as Teshoo Lama's chela is to seek alms, mostly in the form of food and shelter, for his master.

In the person of Teshoo Lama, Kipling brings off the difficult literary feat of creating a genuinely good and religious character who is nevertheless both interesting and likable. In fact, Teshoo Lama's heathen status probably works to Kipling's artistic advantage, since it frees him from the requirement to write about the lama's devoutness in the usual clichés of Victorian Protestant piety.

HE UPSET A BASKET WITH A RED OILSKIN TOP.

OH, FORGIVE ME. I AM CLUMSY.

Mahbub Ali A Pathan horse-trader, a native of what is now Afghanistan. He is also C.25, an intelligence agent working for the British government in India, who employs the boy Kim from time to time as a courier. Mahbub Ali is a Muslim (as Teshoo Lama is Buddhist and Hurree Babu is Hindu). He is a bit of a rogue and a brawler—very much in contrast to the unworldly asceticism of Teshoo Lama—but he shares with Teshoo Lama a concern for Kim's welfare. It is Mahbub Ali who sees Kim's potential as a future player in the Great Game, and encourages the spymaster Creighton Sahib to train him for it.

Hurree Chunder Mukherji ("Hurree Babu") Hurree Babu is a self-described "fearful man," who is at the same time one of the most courageous and resourceful characters in the book, and (as R.17) another player of the Great Game.

A *babu*, in the India of Kipling's time, was a native Bengali clerk or civil servant. The word *babu* is a term of respect, like Mister, rather than a given name, and *Babu-ji* was used in many parts of India to mean "sir." (*Babu* by itself, however, was generally used contemptuously, as signifying a semi-literate native with a mere veneer of modern education.) The stereotypical babu—plump, pedantic, speaking a distinctive stilted and over-elaborate version of English—was a stock figure of British comedy. *Kim* gives us a contrast between the way Hurree Babu is described (and regarded by characters like the two Russian spies), and what he actually does:

> *"He robbed them [the Russian spies]," thought Kim, forgetting his own share in the game. "He tricked them. He lied to them like a Bengali. They give him a chit [a testimonial]. He makes them a mock at the risk of his own life—I would never have gone down to them after the pistol-shots—and then he says that he is a fearful man....And he is a fearful man."*

The widow from Kula (the Sahiba)
A rich old woman, talkative but good-hearted. She takes advantage of the relative freedom given to her by virtue of her age (since she is elderly, the strict rules of purdah—the Hindu practice of keeping women in seclusion—are relaxed somewhat) to travel about India visiting shrines and family members. Kim and Teshoo Lama travel with her for a while in the early days of Kim's adventures; and at the end she provides the place of refuge in which Kim and the lama can recover from their journey into the Himalayan foothills.

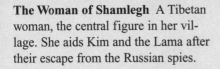

The Woman of Shamlegh A Tibetan woman, the central figure in her village. She aids Kim and the Lama after their escape from the Russian spies.

Colonel Creighton An Englishman working with the Ethnological Survey Department. He is, in addition, a spy-master, running British intelligence in India—Mahbub Ali and Hurree Babu (and eventually Kim) work for him. Acting on Mahbub Ali's recommendation, Creighton directs Kim's education and training as a future spy.

Lurgan Sahib A dealer in jewelry and precious stones. He also works for Creighton, and Kim is sent to him for instruction in some of the more specialized aspects of the intelligence agent's craft, such as makeup and dis-

guise, and the art of memory. He is a faintly sinister and mysterious fellow, a skilled hypnotist who attempts—as a kind of test—to play mind-games with the young Kim. When he attempts to hypnotize Kim into seeing as whole a vase that was broken, Kim resists by using his bilingual ability to think in another language:

So far Kim had been thinking in Hindi, but a tremor came upon him, and, with an effort like that of a swimmer before sharks, who hurls himself out of the water, his mind leaped up from a darkness that was swallowing it and took refuge in—the multiplication-table in English!

Look! It is coming into shape," whispered Lurgan Sahib.

The jar had been smashed—yes, smashed—not the native word, he would not think of that—but smashed—into fifty pieces, and twice three was six, and thrice three was nine, and four times three was twelve. He clung desperately to the repetition. The shadow-outline of the jar cleared like a mist before rubbing eyes. There were the broken shards; there was the spilt water drying in the sun; and through the cracks in the verandah

*showed, all ribbed, the white
house-wall below—and thrice
twelve was thirty-six!*

(This episode also echoes the
lama's comments on the world as
maya, illusion, and the need to see
through that illusion. Kim has the
ability to recognize Lurgan sahib's
hypnotic illusion for what it is; a spir-
itual version of this same recognition
is needed in order to achieve enlightenment.)

PLOT

When the book begins, Kim is
living as a street urchin
in the city of Lahore.
Teshoo Lama arrives in
Lahore, searching for
information on the
whereabouts of the
River of the Arrow. Kim
guides the lama to the
Lahore Museum, and
there eavesdrops on his
conversation with the museum director. He learns that the lama is going to
the city of Benares,
and—mostly for the
fun of it—Kim attaches
himself to the lama as a
chela.

At the same time
the Pathan horse-dealer
Mahbub Ali, in his role
as a spy for the English
government, comes to
Lahore with a report
that must get to the

spymaster Colonel Creighton in the
town of Umballa, on the way to
Benares. Mahbub Ali also has enemy
agents hot on his trail (working, pre-
sumably, for Russia—the "sympathetic
Northern Power," as the book calls it).
Rather than risk losing the report to
them, he gives it to Kim to deliver.

Kim delivers the report, and con-
tinues on his journeys with Teshoo
Lama. They come across an encamp-
ment of the Mavericks—Kim's father's
regiment, and Kim is caught eaves-
dropping outside their tents. His birth-
certificate and his father's Masonic
papers, which he carries with him as a
sort of charm, serve to establish his
identity, and the two
chaplains of the regi-
ment propose to do
their duty by sending
him away to school.

Teshoo Lama and
Mahbub Ali intervene
to save him. The lama
provides the money
which will buy Kim a
first-class education at the school of
St. Xavier in Partibus in Lucknow
(rather than the chari-
ty education an
orphan would usually
get.) And Mahbub Ali
enlists Colonel
Creighton's efforts on
Kim's behalf, on the
grounds that Kim will
someday make an
excellent player in the
Great Game. Kim is,
accordingly, given

Kipling and Freemasonry

Freemasonry was (and still is) one of the largest and most widely established fraternal orders in the world. Its beginnings lie in the craft guilds of the middle ages, when the masons were, literally, stonecutters, employed in building the castles and cathedrals of the age. As the medieval era drew to a close, the masons' guilds began to admit others—usually men of wealth and social status—and gradually transformed themselves from an organization of working stonemasons and builders into societies devoted to general ideals such as fraternity, equality, and peace. These ideals, combined with a spirit of religious toleration and a belief in basic equality of all people, made the societies increasingly popular during the 18th century. In England, four or more such guilds, or lodges, united in 1717 to form a grand lodge for London and Westminster, which shortly became the Grand Lodge of England—the "mother" grand lodge of Freemasons in the world, from which are derived all the official grand lodges.

Kipling was a Freemason, and Masonic ideals and images occur repeatedly in Kipling's work. In *Captains Courageous*, for example,

the American sailor Tom Platt is able to communicate with sailors from the French fishing fleet on the Grand Banks by virtue of their Masonic brotherhood. The short story "The Man Who Would Be King" also draws heavily on Masonic lore. In *Kim*, it is Kim's father's Freemasonry (plus the good offices of a Catholic chaplain and the money from Teshoo Lama) that saves Kim from being brought up as a regimental orphan—a regimen which, however well-meaning it might have been, would have stifled the boy's free spirit.

Kipling also uses Masonic imagery to emphasize his own thematic concerns throughout his work—in particular, the idea of an essential brotherhood, transcending race and creed and class, among men who share a common goal, skill, or profession. He uses this imagery to convey, among other things, the brotherhood-in-arms of the soldiers in the British Army in the poem "The Widow at Windsor" (the title refers to Queen Victoria):

> *"Then 'ere's to the Lodge o' the Widow,*
>
> *From the Pole to the Tropics it runs—*

> To the Lodge that we tile
> with the rank an' the file,
>   And open in form with
> the guns."

("Tiling" and "opening in form" are both references to Masonic rituals.)

In *Kim*, the bonds of a shared profession or enthusiasm reach across racial and religious lines and tie together the director of the Lahore museum and Teshoo Lama, both scholars of the life of Buddha. Likewise, Colonel Creighton and Hurree Babu share a ambition to become Fellows of the Royal Society:

> No money and no prefer-
> ment would have drawn
> Creighton from his work on
> the Indian Survey, but deep in
> his heart also lay an ambi-
> tion to write "F. R. S." after
> his name. Honours of a sort
> he knew could be obtained by
> ingenuity and the help of
> friends, but, to the best of his
> belief, nothing save work—
> papers representing a life of
> it—took a man into the
> Society which he had bom-
> barded for years with mono-
> graphs on strange Asiatic
> cults and unknown cus-
> toms....So Creighton smiled,
> and thought better of Hurree
> Babu, moved by like desires.

Kim himself, by the end of the novel, has become an initiate into yet another brotherhood, the brotherhood of the players of the Great Game—those who are known to the government only by their numbers, and who have prices on their heads, and who are beyond the government's protection: "If we die, we die. Our names are blotted from the book. That is all."

training as a future spy in addition to his regular education.

At the conclusion of Kim's schooling, when he is seventeen, he's sent out to spend a half-year traveling with Teshoo Lama (getting "de-Englished," as Hurree Babu puts it) before beginning his official employment. On the road, he encounters a fellow-agent (E.23) who is being pursued by enemies, and helps him to disguise himself and escape. Then Kim and Teshoo Lama head up into the Himalayan foothills, still searching for the River of the Arrow.

Along the way they encounter Hurree Babu, who is also searching for something—in his case, for a pair of foreign "sportsmen" (a Frenchman and a Russian—more spies, of course) in order to insinuate himself into their entourage and steal their maps and papers.

When the sportsmen are found, there is an accidental confrontation: one of the two men tears Teshoo Lama's drawing of the Wheel of Life, and—when the lama grows angry—strikes him. A fight follows, and in the mass confusion Kim is able to steal the papers, while Hurree Babu distracts the foreigners and leads them away. After that, however, Kim faces a long and wearing journey down out of the foothills, burdened by responsibility both for the delivery of the stolen papers, and for the welfare of the rapidly failing Teshoo Lama.

At last he brings Teshoo Lama safely to the home of the widow of Kula, an old and wealthy woman who had befriended Kim and the lama during their first journey together. Here Kim collapses with exhaustion. Upon his recovery, he finds that both Hurree Babu and Mahbub Ali are now at Kula, and he is able to hand over the papers. He also learns that the lama (by means of a vision after nearly drowning in a nearby stream) has at last found the River of the Arrow for which he has been searching.

THE RUSSIAN STRUCK THE OLD MAN FULL IN THE FACE.

BACKGROUND
The British in India

British rule in India began as a commercial venture. In 1600, the "Governor and Company of Merchants of London trading into the East Indies"—commonly known as the East India Company—was founded by Queen Elizabeth I. Its purpose was to take up some of the lucrative trade in spices enjoyed at that time by the Portuguese and the Dutch. For some time the Company did no more than sponsor regular trading voyages between England and India; but as time passed it began building storehouses on the Indian mainland, and then forts to protect the storehouses, and from there, inevitably, settlements around the forts. Madras in 1639, Bombay in 1668, and Calcutta in 1686 all became centers of activity for the East India Company.

India at that time was experiencing a period of political instability. The Mogul empire, which had controlled the greater part of India for almost two centuries, had fallen into decay, and was fragmenting into smaller kingdoms and principalities. Although the Dutch and the Portuguese had been squeezed out of the Indian trade, by the mid-1700s the French had begun to pursue it aggressively. The British East India Company, always in the interest of protecting its ports and its trade, made alliances and waged war in response—and, over the course of the next century and a half, found itself moving bit by bit into the power vacuum left by the fall of the Moguls.

By the middle of the 19th century, England, as embodied by the East India Company, was the paramount power over most of the Indian subcontinent. Independent states that would not make treaties with the English were often invaded under one pretext or another; states where the ruler had no direct male heir were annexed by the English, a move which went against the local custom by which a childless ruler could adopt an heir. The mood of the people in general, in the face of these policies, was suspicious and resentful.

It was at that point, in 1857, that the English in India made a public relations error of staggering proportions. The East India Company decided to issue new and improved rifle cartridges to its *sepoys*, or native troops. Part of the drill for loading and firing required the trooper to rip the cartridge open with his teeth—a cartridge that was wrapped in greased paper. The cartridges were said to be greased with a mixture of beef and pork fat, making them repugnant both to the Hindu troopers (for whom cows were sacred) and to the Moslems (for whom pigs were unclean). This was assumed to be a deliberate measure introduced to break the caste of the sepoys and force them to adopt English ways. Ordered to accept and use the new cartridges, the troops of the garrison at Meerut mutinied, killing their officers, and sepoys all over India soon followed their example.

The Indian Mutiny (also known as the Sepoy Rebellion) was brief but vicious, marked by atrocities committed on both sides. In the end, the English were able to re-assert their control, but the East India Company's rule was over. In 1858 the administration of English territory in India passed into the direct control of the English Crown (represented by a governor-general, or viceroy.)

This new regime endured for almost a century, and was in force during the time of Kipling's *Kim*. The greater part of India was divided into British territories ruled directly by England. The rest of the country was broken up into (theoretically) semi-independent native states whose rulers held power more or less by permission of the British government. And on the borders of India, especially to the north and to the west, lay the frontier states whose obedience to English rule was always hard to enforce—and where the Great Game of political espionage was played for the highest stakes.

The "Great Game"

When Kipling wrote of the Great Game, he meant the veiled struggle between England and Russia on the borders of India. Russia's 19th-century expansionism, combined with its long-established desire for a reliable warm-water seaport, made northern and western India into a tempting target. The area being contested also included Afghanistan and the Khyber Pass, an important gateway on the route between Afghanistan and Pakistan (then still a part of India).

Since England and Russia had—theoretically—been at peace since the Crimean War in 1853-1856, the warfare was carried out secretly, by means of spies and informers and the use of local Indian rulers as cat's-paws and proxies. The plot that Mahbub Ali brings news of in the opening chapters of *Kim* is typical:

"But, recently, five confederated Kings, who had no business to confederate, had been informed by a kindly Northern Power [i.e., Russia] *that there was a leakage of news from their territories into British India....And there was that on Mahbub Ali which he did not wish to keep an hour longer than was necessary—a wad of closely folded tissue-paper, wrapped in oil-skin—an impersonal, unaddressed statement, with five microscopic pin-holes in one corner, that most scandalously betrayed the five confederated Kings, the sympathetic Northern Power, a Hindu banker in Peshawur, a firm of gun-makers in Belgium, and an important, semi-independent Mohammedan ruler to the south."*

The English response, as determined by the Commander-in-Chief, is also typical:

"Warn the Pindi and Peshawur brigades. It will disorganize all the summer reliefs, but we can't help that. This comes of not smashing them thoroughly the first time. Eight thousand should be enough....It's punishment, not war."

For the most part, however, the struggle was carried out not by armies, but by spies for one side or the other—men like Mahbub Ali and Hurree Babu and the man known only by his number, E.23 (like many another fictional agent after him). This is the game that Kim's polyglot, multicultural childhood has made him admirably suited to play, and for which his teachers (with the exception of Teshoo Lama) have trained him.

Britain no longer rules India, and the Czars no longer rule Russia, but the geographic factors that lay behind their secret warfare remain the same. Countries like Afghanistan, Pakistan, and Tibet remain areas of strategic importance to powerful and antagonistic countries outside their borders—the prize now is access to oil reserves, as well as to warm-water seaports and potential trade and invasion routes—and the Great Game, in one form or another, is still played.

The Eightfold Path

The Indian subcontinent was, and is, home to many different religions, of which Hinduism is the majority belief. In Kipling's day, Islam also was one of the major Indian religions, though after the coming of Independence this changed—the majority of Muslims lived in the territories which later became Pakistan and (eventually) Bangladesh. The religion which plays the greatest role in *Kim*, however, is Buddhism—specifically, the Tibetan Buddhism of Kim's mentor Teshoo Lama. It's impossible to give a complete account of the Buddhist religion here, but a few key points are helpful for a reader of Kim to know.

WHEN WE RETURNED HERE I TOOK NO FOOD, I DRANK NO WATER FOR TWO DAYS AND NIGHTS. MY SOUL WENT FREE AS AN EAGLE. I SAW THE RIVER OF THE ARROW AT MY FEET AND, DESCENDING, THE WATERS OF IT CLOSED OVER ME. AND BEHOLD, I WAS FREE FROM SIN, AND THOU SHALT BE, ALSO.

Siddhartha Gautama (known later as the Buddha, or Enlightened One) was born in India in the year 563 B.C. He was the son of the ruler of a petty kingdom, and later legends said that the omens surrounding his birth indicated he was destined to become either a sage or the ruler of an empire. At the age of 29, he abandoned his life of luxury and set out on a quest for peace and enlightenment, seeking release from the cycle of rebirths. For several years he lived a life of severe asceticism, attempting to achieve enlightenment through self-denial. When this approach brought him no closer to enlightenment, he abandoned it as fruitless, and adopted a middle path between the life of indulgence and that of self-denial. It was at that point, while sitting in meditation under a bo tree, that he rose through a series of higher states of consciousness and at last attained the enlightenment for which he had been searching. After this experience, the Buddha spent the rest of his life in preaching and wandering from place to place, gathering a body of disciples who further carried out the spread of his teachings after his death.

The core of these teachings can be summed up in the Four Noble Truths:

•First, that life is suffering. Even death brings no relief, for the Buddha accepted the Hindu idea of life as cyclical, with death leading to further rebirth.

•Second, that all suffering is caused by ignorance of the nature of reality and by the craving, attachment, and grasping that result from such ignorance. As Teshoo Lama says, when he fears that he will be parted from Kim by the plans of the regimental chaplains for the boy's schooling:

> *"And I am a follower of the Way," he said bitterly. "The sin is mine and the punishment is mine. I made believe to myself—for I see now that it was but make-belief—that thou wast sent to me to aid me in the Search. So my heart went out to thee for thy charity and*

thy courtesy and the wisdom of thy little years. But those who follow the Way must permit not the fire of any desire or attachment, for all that is illusion"

• Third, that suffering can be ended by overcoming ignorance and attachment.

• And fourth, that the way to end suffering is by the Eightfold Path: right views, right intention, right speech, right action, right livelihood, right effort, right-mindedness, and right contemplation.

Tibetan Buddhism, or Lamaism (from the Tibetan word *blama*, meaning "superior"), is a combination of Buddhism and the ritualistic shamanism which had been native to the area prior to the coming of Buddhism. Teshoo Lama speaks of how Buddhist practices in Tibet have diverged from what he sees as their original purity:

"...it was in my mind that the Old Law was not well followed; being overlaid, as thou knowest, with devildom, charms, and idolatry. . . The books of my lamassery I read, and they were dried pith; and the later ritual with which we of the Reformed Law have cumbered ourselves—that, too, had no worth to these old eyes. Even the followers of the Excellent One are at feud

on feud with one another. It is all illusion. Ay, Maya, illusion."

Tying together the diverse plot elements in *Kim*, as they tied together the diverse regions and cultures of British India, are images of life and travel on the Grand Trunk Road and the Indian Railway, both products of British rule. (The railway figures largely in Kim's life from the very beginning: Kim's father leaves his regiment and takes a job on the railway instead, and Kim spends the first three years of his life riding up and down the line.)

The close quarters of a third-class railway car make neighbors and traveling companions of people who would not normally come in contact with one another. On Kim's first journey with Teshoo Lama from Lahore to Umballa, the two of them find places in a railway car that also holds a Sikh artisan, a prosperous Hindu farmer with his wife and child, a Hindu moneylender, a courtesan from Amritsar, and a sepoy (a native soldier in the Indian army). The conversation in the railway car touches specifically upon how the

railroad brings people together and breaks down caste barriers:

> "I say," began the money-lender, pursing his lips, "that there is not one rule of right living that these te-rains do not cause us to break. We sit, for example, side by side with all castes and peoples."

Later in the same conversation, when the Sikh artisan and the sepoy are on the verge of disagreement, the idea of a brotherhood transcending caste is also raised explicitly by the woman from Amritsar:

> "Nay, but all who serve the Sirkar [the British government in India] with weapons in their hands are, as it were, one brotherhood. There is one brotherhood of the caste, but beyond that again"—she looked round timidly "— the bond of the Pulton—the Regiment—eh?"

In such a mixed company, a Tibetan holy man and his *chela* are just two more passengers, and nobody finds their presence odd. Later, on another railway journey, Kim disguises the fugitive intelligence agent E.23 as a *saddhu* (a Hindu ascetic, seeking for enlightenment through various extreme forms of self-denial and mortification), and the idea of a *saddhu* with a train ticket meets with the same acceptance.

The Grand Trunk Road, upon which Kim and Teshoo Lama make some of their later journeys, allows for a similar mingling. The road was part of a series of military highways built by the Moguls, and runs across the northern part of the Indian subcontinent from Peshawur, in what is now Pakistan, to Calcutta in Bengal. The road and its history, and the benefits it bestows, are described for Teshoo Lama—and for the reader—by an aged veteran of the Indian army, an old soldier whose memories go back to the days of the Sepoy Rebellion:

> "And now we come to the Big Road," said he...."It is long since I have ridden this way, but thy boy's talk stirred me. See, Holy One—the Great Road, which is the backbone of all Hind [India]. For the most part it is shaded, as here, with four lines of trees; the middle road—all hard—takes the quick traffic. In the days before rail-carriages the Sahibs traveled up and down here in hundreds. Now there are only country-carts and such like. Left and right is the rougher road for the heavy carts—grain and cotton and timber, bhoosa, lime, and hides. A man goes in safety here—for at every few kos is a police-station. The police are thieves and extortioners (I myself would patrol it with cavalry—young recruits under a strong captain), but at least they do not suffer any rivals. All castes and kinds of men move here. Look! Brahmins and chumars, bankers and tinkers, barbers